John Lees Courtenay

Juvenile Poems

John Lees Courtenay

Juvenile Poems

ISBN/EAN: 9783337368715

Printed in Europe, USA, Canada, Australia, Japan

Cover: Foto ©Andreas Hilbeck / pixelio.de

More available books at **www.hansebooks.com**

JUVENILE POEMS,

BY THE LATE

JOHN COURTENAY, *Jun.*

———————

WITH

An Elegy on his Death.

———

Nos juvenem exanimum, et nil jam cœleſtibus ullis
Debentem, vano mœſti comitamur honore.

VIRG.

———————

London :

PRINTED BY J. JONES, CHAPEL STREET, SOHO.

1795.

ELEGY,

TO THE MEMORY OF

JOHN COURTENAY,

A CADET IN THE CORPS OF ENGINEERS, WHO
DIED AT CALCUTTA, DECEMBER, 1794,

IN THE NINETEENTH YEAR OF HIS AGE.

— — — Οὔτε μοι ἠὼς
Ἡδεῖ, ἀτ' ἀκτὶς ὠκέθ' ἠελίου.

O SHADE belov'd, ftill prefent to my fight,
My daily vifion, and my dream by night!
In all thy youthful bloom thou feem'ft to rife,
With filial love yet beaming from thy eyes.
Such were thy looks, and fuch thy manly grace,
When late I held thee in a laft embrace;
When in my breaft prefaging terrors grew,
And funk in grief, I figh'd a long adieu.
How foon to thee this plaintive note I owe,
My plaintive note to footh maternal woe!

B

" * Thefe fading orbs their darling view no more,
" And the laft charm of ebbing life is o'er."
Dark o'er my head the louring moments roll,
For ever fet the fun-beam of my foul.

    Is this indeed the univerfal doom,
No ray of hope to cheer the lonely tomb !
Perhaps the foul, a pure æthereal flame,
May ftill furvive her frail and tranfient frame;
And rapt in blifs the great Creator trace,
Celeftial power who lives thro' boundlefs fpace !
See his benevolence unclouded fhine,
Where wifdom, virtue dwell in joys divine ;
Search Truths fublime, with facred rapture fcan,
His gracious views conceal'd from erring man:
But reafon vainly would this depth explore,
And fabled fyftems make us doubt the more.

    O Youth belov'd, now mouldering in the tomb,
Each foft progreffion even to manhood's bloom,
My fancy paints ; in infancy my pride,
With fparkling eyes ftill playful at my fide ;
The lively boy then rofe with winning grace,
Till rip'ning ardour mark'd his glowing face.

* In the Elegy on Captain COURTENAY.

I faw him fhine in every liberal art,
Science and Fame the paffion of his heart.
Where GRANTA's domes o'erhang the cloifter'd plain,
Studious he mix'd in learning's penfive train;
There, Meditation lent her facred aid,
To woo bright fcience in the peaceful fhade;
Why tempt that burning clime, that fatal fhore?
* The glorious motive pains my bofom more.

When bards fublime attun'd the founding lyre,
His vivid breaft difplay'd congenial fire.
He bade TYRTÆUS' martial ardour fhine,
And breathes his fpirit in each glowing line.
With HENRY's glory gilds his claffic lays,
And joins the Prince's in the hero's praife.
Indignant fcorn on freedom's foe he flings,
And fpurns ambition the mean vice of kings.
With PRIOR's graceful eafe he moves along,
And laughs at fiction in his fportive fong.
With pregnant fancy, brilliant wit defines,
And blends examples in his playful lines.
In fprightly numbers chants † MARIA's fway,
While WALLER's ‡ groves refound the amorous lay.

* Extract of one of his letters from Portfmouth, April 20th, 1794.—
" For the idea of being a fervice to, and of again feeing thofe who are fo
" dear to me, is the moft lively and pleafing fenfation I can ever have."
† Verfes addreffed to Mifs M. L.   ‡ Written at Hall-Barn, Beconsfield.

How pleas'd with mine to mix thy * tuneful ftrain,
When Freedom's banner wav'd on GALLIA's plain;
There, † fervid courage won thee early praife,
And wing'd with pleafure flew our happy days:
Never did Nature's bounteous hand impart,
A nobler fpirit, or a gentler heart.

How dear to all!—by focial love refin'd,
No felfifh paffion warp'd his generous mind!
When from my breaft, a figh reluctant ftole,
That fpoke the boding forrows of my foul;
He grafp'd my hand, the parting moment nigh,
A filial tear yet ftarting from his eye;
And fweetly ftrove the prefcient gloom to cheer,
Thefe words for ever vibrate on my ear.
" Ah why repine, the palm by honour won,
" Defcends a bright incentive to thy fon,
" To fpurn at wealth in India's tempting clime,
" If ftain'd by bribes, if fully'd by a crime.

---

* The REPUBLICAN, and NUNS Song, publifhed in the Poetical
Epiftles from France, &c.

† A very young foldier at the door of the National Convention menaced
him with his pointed bayonet, which he inftantly feized, and wrefted the
piece out of his hands.—One of the members was fortunately a witnefs of
the tranfaction, and after reprimanding the centinel, introduced my fon into
the Convention, and told me the fact, with high eulogiums on his fpirit.

" O, let my voice each anxious care difpell,
" I'll foon return to thofe I love fo well."

That promis'd blifs,—that vital beam is paſt;
Hope's genial fhoots, all withered by one blaſt.
He'll ne'er return in fhining talents bleſt,
With duteous zeal to glad a parent's breaſt.
'Midſt focial joy, in feſtive pleafure gay,
A fudden * corfe, the blooming victim lay.
While here forlorn, I yet exiſt to tell,
How in the glow of youth my darling fell.
Life's clofing fcenes no confolation lend,
† I've loſt my fweet companion and my friend.—
That grief is vain,—but tempts me to repine,
Ev'n ‡ Fox's generous tears have flow'd with mine.

---

* Capt. Grey, to R. J. Efq.——" In anfwer to your note of
" yeſterday, I am compelled to the painful taſk of communicating the
" melancholly acconnt of Mr. C——'s death. At a ball the 14th of
" December, being overheated with dancing, he imprudently drank a
" glafs of lemonade, which proved almoſt inſtantly fatal."

† Extract of a letter:——Cambridge, February 10th, 1792.—" I
" am more obliged to you, than I can exprefs: grateful I am to my
" Father, and ever fhall remain; paffion may at times have led me
" aftray, yet ſtill did I ever remember his kindnefs and affection, ad-
" mire his talents, refpect him as a parent, and love him as a protector,
" a companion, and a friend "

‡ Mr. Fox, with generous and confoling attention, and with that
fympathizing friendfhip which diſtinguifh him, gave me the firſt intima-
tion of this fatal event.

O fhade benign, ftill at my couch arife,
Till low in earth, thy once lov'd Father lies.
Ne'er from my mind can thy memorial part,
Thy picture's grav'd for ever on my heart:
But India's mould contains thy hallow'd fhrine;
Vain my laft wifh to mix my duft with thine.
For thee, fweet EMMA drops the tender tear,
Sighs o'er thy verfe, and thy untimely bier;
For thee, SOPHIA heaves her aching breaft,
While plaintively fhe lulls her babe to reft.
For thee, thy MOTHER's eyes inceffant flow;
Thy fate alone could touch my heart with woe.
With flowers I'll ftrew thy urn, and clafp thy buft;
With my laft numbers confecrate thy duft:
Dwell on thy praife, and feel while life remains,
The joy of grief from thy harmonious ftrains.
Still to thy fhade each facred honour pay,
And to thy grave devote the mournful lay.
'Tis Nature's charm to eafe the troubl'd breaft,
And footh the anguifh of the foul to reft;
We fondly hope, by dear delufion led,
To wake our own fenfations in the dead;
By fympathy reverfe the eternal doom,
Revive the clay, and animate the tomb.

BATH, AUGUST, 1791.

HENRICI QUINTI LAUDES.

REGIS HENRICI, mihi da, benigna
Artibus belli variifq' pacis
Dulcis inſtructi, reſonare Muſa
    Splendida facta,

Qui manu parvâ comitatus, agros
Galliæ pingues populavit, atq'
Copias vicit numero carentes
    Marte cruento.——

Ille per turmas facie ſerenâ
Ivit exhortans ſocios laborum
Fortiter pugnam pueris, inire
    Conjugibuſq'.

Quamvis in terram cecidit tremendis
Ictibus multis superatus hostis,
Vicit at cunctos tamen imperator
  Ense potenti.

Plurimas gentes trepidas subegit
Nescius vinci Macedo superbus,
Gallicam gentem domuit ferocem.
  Anglicus heros.

Sub duce hoc magno intrepidi Britanni
Usq' pugnabant veluti leones,
Atq' fugerunt pavidi timore
  Semper ab illis.

Galliæ vastæ populi frequentes;
Sic lupum vitant pecudes rapacem
Quando nocturnam stabulos lacessit
  Quærere prædam.

Dumq' regnâsset generosus heros
Classe Gallorum Genuæ q' victâ,
Angliæ nati domini fuere
  Æquoris omnis.

* In mero gaudet dapibus, jocifq'
Filius regis folio fedentis,
Et fuas femper dominis venuftis
    .   Præterit horas.

Hoc modo Henricus levis atq' vixit;
Sed citò mores juvenis reliquit,
Regiam fedem decorabit atq'
    GEORGIUS almus.

* For him, the feftive board had charms,
    Where wit and humour fhine :
And yielding beauty bleft his arms,
    Amidft the joys of wine.

But fee the fcepter'd hero reign,
    His youthful foibles flown ;
Thus, Fame's loud plaudits GEORGE fhall gain,
    And glorious fill the throne.

BATH, SEPTEMBER 2, 1791.

HORA TERTIA, P. M.

———————

ANXIAS curas animis fugate,
Gaudeat quifque hac redeunte luce,
Qua dies noftri numerat fluentes
          Sanguinis Auctor.

Hanc diem fauftam, properate cuncti,
Cum bono vino celebrare, curas
Quod ftatim folvit; facit atq' noftra
          Pectora læta.

Prandium jamjam famuli miniftrant
Alteram veftem induere et neceffe eft,
Non mihi, quamvis cupio, licet nunc
          Scribere plura.

EXULTING, tune the choral lay,
 Bid anxious care retire ;
With pride I hail this happy day,
 The birth-day of our Sire.

To me this genial morn is dear,
 Propitious may it shine ;
And bring us each revolving year,
 The joys of mirth of wine.

But see, the festive hour is nigh,
 The servants haste along;
To dress myself, I'm forc'd to fly,
 And leave the unfinish'd song.

JUS DEPONENDI, ET ELIGENDI, REGES, EX LITERIS SACRIS DEMONSTRATUM.

QUUM Deus ex cælo Judæis munera mifit,
Tunc jus pofcebant folio deponere Regem;
Audivit fanctus mox vota ardentia vates,
Dejecit numen, SAULUM regemqu' creavit;
Congruit electu gentis fic rector Olympic;—
Sed pius * EDMUNDUS populi nunc jura recufat!

A CLASSICAL APOLOGY FOR PHYSICIANS.

ÆSCULAPIUS of yore (as in ftory we 're told),
Was fo fond of his fees, that a handful of gold,
Induc'd him a carcafe to life to reftore,
Altho' fuch a CURE was ne'er heard of before.
Whereupon thund'ring Jove threw a bolt at his head,
And on Pluto's remonftrance, the Doctor lay dead.
From hence 'tis aver'd how phyficians of late,
That they may not fuffer a fimilar fate;
Inftead of reftoring to life the deceas'd,
Are content if by them, men from life are releas'd.

* BURKE's Reflections.

TRANSLATIONS

FROM THE

WAR ELEGIES OF TYRTÆUS.

———

— — — Infignis Homerus,
Tyrtæufq' mares animos in martia bella,
Verfibus exacuit.

———

ELEGY THE FIRST.

I SCORN to fing the active racer's praife,
Nor deem him worthy of a poet's lays ;
Not tho' in fwiftnefs he outftript the fteed,
Or e'en furpafs'd the Thracian wind in fpeed.
Nor would I honour, or tranfmit to fame,
The brawny wreftler's undeferving name ;
Not tho' in bulk he match'd the Cyclops race,
Boafted the beauties of Tithonus face :
No,—not if fortune with benignant hand,
Had given him Pelop's empire to command,
Pour'd down the wealth of Midas on his head,
The ftores of Cinyras before him fpread.

Nor if kind Heaven had on his tongue beſtow'd,
Thoſe charms of ſpeech that from Adraſtus flow'd.
Not, tho' he Fortune's richeſt gifts poſſeſs'd,
Unleſs true courage fir'd his manly breaſt.
Say,—is he worthy to enjoy the light
Whoſe ſpirit fails him in the arduous fight?
Who dares not boldly at his poſt to ſtand,
And wield his falchion 'mid the hoſtile band.

Honour's the nobleſt prize a man can gain,
The brighteſt laurel he can e'er obtain ;
Then let each warrior emulate his fire,
Let Sparta's glory every ſoul inſpire.
See the youth ſpring impetuous on the foe,
And deal deſtruction in each fatal blow:
He ſcorns to yield, to tremble, or to fly,
But thinks it glorious in the field to die.
Now fires his countrymen to manly deeds,
And the firm hoſt to fame and conqueſt leads.
For lo ! where ſcatter'd, ſtruck with wild affright,
The routed phalanx turn their ſteps to flight.
'Twas HE, that drove them from the duſty plain,
He pierc'd their ranks, and broke their marſhal'd train.
At length he falls,—falls and reſigns his breath,
And in his country's cauſe, exults in death.

The well form'd breaſt plate, and the ſhield are found,
Streaming with blood, and hack'd with many a wound.
The young, the old attend his funeral bier,
Shed o'er his mangled corſe a generous tear;
His infant children ſhare their father's fame,
While, all reſpect, and venerate his name.
And tho' in earth his mould'ring bones are laid,
Yet ſtill with glory are his deeds repay'd;
Recording ages ſhall with pleaſure tell,
" He bravely for his country fought and fell."
—But if he meet not this heroic fate,
He ſtands the glorious pillar of the ſtate,
The young, the old, the warlike chief admire,
Applaud his valour, and his patriot fire.
Then ye who wiſh the victor's palm to gain,
Who thirſt the wreath of merit to obtain;
Ruſh—ruſh to war, gird on the ſhining ſteel,
And fight like heroes for the common weal.

ELEGY THE SECOND.

HOW long ye cowards will ye fenfelefs ftand,
While war and famine vex your native land!
Still—ftill inactive, hide your heads for fhame,
Blind to your anceftors illuftrious fame!
And can ye tremble, to refign this life,
The infant fhielding and the tender wife.
For know—we all muft die, or foon or late,
So Fate commands, and all muft yield to fate.

Then draw your fwords, uprear your blazing crefts,
And bear your glitt'ring fhields before your breafts.
Oft from the battle's rage, the coward flies,
But Fate arrefts him, and at home he dies.—
But mark the intrepid hero's glorious end,
The people's champion, and the people's friend.
When dead, by all lamented and deplor'd,
By all when living, reverenc'd and ador'd.
As yon proud trophy wins admiring eyes,
So with bright laurels crown'd behold him rife;
His grateful country's bulwark, pride and boaft,
In him tho' fingle, they poffefs a hoft.—

ELEGY THE THIRD.

SPARTANS—ye chofen fav'rites of the fky,
See Jove propitious thunder from on high.
Then let each warrior grafp his ample fhield,
Nor fhun the hoftile throng that crouds the field,
Who dreads for freedom to refign his breath?
Who in his country's caufe will fhrink from death?
How oft the battle's rage have ye endur'd,
To all the horrors of grim war inur'd!
Oft on your foes the furious onfet made,
And hurl'd their fquadrons to the Stygian fhade!
—But now the buckler's drop'd, your fpirit's fled,
Your army routed, and your heroes dead.—
Hafte—form the phalanx, all your powers combine,
And in the van, like Spartan foldiers fhine;
When thus united, none can ftand your force,
Flight is the coward's hope, his fole refource.—
Your's be the glory of the bloody day,
While trembling wretches fkulk with fhame away.
Bafe is the man who wounds a flying foe,
Bafe is the man who aims a treacherous blow.

Bold be your fight, difpel each childifh fear,
And in the combat, fierce as Wolves appear.
Brandifh your fwords, and couch the quiv'ring lance,
Now ftretch your fpears, and to the charge advance.
Then hand to hand, let each a foe engage,
Strain every nerve, and fummon all your rage :
Let fword meet fword, and breaft oppofe to breaft,
Shield clafh with fhield, and creft contend with creft.

Ye light arm'd foldiers whirl the leathern fling,
Speed the quick dart, the rocky fragment fling ;
So fh ll your toils with victory be crown'd,
And Sparta's fons for ever be renown'd.——

ELEGY THE FOURTH.

THE man who falls, when fighting to defend,
His country's freedom, meets a glorious end.

But if by poverty deprefs'd he roam,
Far from his native city, and his home ;

He meanly fues a pittance to obtain,
To feed his tender wife, and infant train;
A mother and a fire his cares engage,
Worn down by grief, and funk in helplefs age.
Thus doom'd to fuffer indigence, difgrace,
His name difhonour'd, and defpifed his race;
To want's fharp pangs and mifery a prey,
'Till death in pity fnatch the wretch away.

Then be it ours, my friends, the foe to wait,
Of life regardlefs, and the ftorms of fate;
Here, with your fhields an iron rampart raife,
And fire your fouls by glorious thirft of praife.
The coward trembles, and the coward flies,
The hero conquers, or he bravely dies.

Guard the old warrior ev'n in weaknefs brave,
Snatch him from danger, from deftruction fave;
Oh piteous fight, to view the pointed dart,
Transfix his breaft, and pierce his dauntlefs heart.
While vigorous youths to flight for fafety truft,
And fee the veteran hero fink in duft.—

ODE ADDRESSED TO EMMA,

OCCASONED BY MY FATHER'S ODE, ADDRESSED
TO TWO YOUNG LADIES, ON THEIR
RETURN FROM ITALY.

━━━━━━━━━━━

Je fuis enchanté,
    Par l'hereufe varieté
La racherche, la nouveauté
    Et la noblefse de fes rimes.

Que j'aime aufsi la netteté
    Le ton precis dent il s'exprime,
Quelle rare fecondité
    D'images riantes fublimes.

━━━━━━━━━━━

B L E S T with a true Horatian fire,
The Poet ftrikes the founding lyre,
    The blue ey'd maid he fings;
Paternal love infpires his lays,
He fondly chaunts his EMMA's praife,
    And fweeps the yielding ftrings.

Now with fuperior art pourtray'd,
The various beauties are difplay'd,

That grace the Hefperian land;
Borne on triumphant fancy's wings,
The Bard in tuneful numbers fings,
    And fhews a mafter's hand.

O'er all his fmooth melodious lines,
A warm imagination fhines,
    And beams of fancy play;
Tho' * ADDISON from Tiber wrote,
Yet not fo rapturous his note,
    So claffical his lay.

As Vulcan o'er Æneas' fhield,
Rome's future eminence reveal'd,
    (Vers'd in the rolls of fate)
And wrought in gold with art divine,
The heroes of illuftrious line,
    That prop'd the Roman ftate.

So in the Poet's pleafing ftrains,
The Emprefs of the world remains,

---

* The candid reader (efpecially if he be a father) will excufe the
juvenile criticifm of a fon, prejudiced by partiality and affection.

Resplendent to our view ;
By the inspiring muse impel'd,
He paints what ne'er his eyes beheld,
        Yet still the picture's true.

But now to Belgia's shore I fly,
And see joy sparkle in your eye,
        While ardent wishes rise ;
When quick you fly Batavia's plain,
And launch into the Eastern main,
        To seek your native skies.

O may the broad, the flowing sails,
Expanded by auspicious gales,
        Catch every gentle breeze ;
Ye waves propitious lend your aid,
Safe to convey the blue ey'd maid,
        And waft her o'er the seas.

Behold she comes (her Father's pride)
SOPHIA blooming by her side,
        With mild expressive face ;
See the fond sisters arm in arm,
By sweet affection blend each charm,
        And shine with mutual grace.

Each foft enchanting finile combin'd,
With eafy manners, tafte refin'd,
　　Sophia's charms difclofe;
In love's chafte tye, long may fhe fhare,
The fond delight, the pleafing care,
　　That nuptial blifs beftows.

From Emma, Humour's native ftrain,
And Wit's enliv'ning happy vein,
　　In brilliant fallies fhoot;
As thro' the verdant foliage glow,
And on one ftem, engrafted grow,
　　Two different forts of fruit.

TO MISS M*** L****.

WITH A COPY OF MR. FOX'S VERSES TO MRS. CREW.

———————

Ne vous offenſez pas,
Si je vous pretends vous plaire;
Je ne peux me taire.

———————

IF bleſs'd with Fox's tuneful vein,
 MARIA's charms I'd ſing;
To her addreſs my ardent ſtrain,
 And wake the trembling ſtring.—

Her cheeks diſcloſe the crimſon bloom,
 That paints the ſcented roſe;
Her breath exhales the mild perfume,
 The air in which IT grows.

How can I chant the graceful fair,
 In beauty's luftre bright !
To what fhall I her eyes compare,
 That beam celeftial light !—

As wildly mutable they roll,
 We feel their boundlefs fway;
We bow beneath their fweet controul,
 And love, admire, obey.

Thofe brilliant orbs inflame mankind,
 Thence, CUPID fires our hearts;
And as the unerring boy is blind,
 By THEM directs his darts.

What Bard fuch dazzling charms can fing,
 In youth's refplendent glow;
Could ev'n TITIAN radiance fling,
 O'er yon Cærulean bow?

COWLEY'S ODE ON WIT,

PARAPHRASED *.

TELL me, tell me what is WIT,
Ye who dealers are in it?
Variety it ftill affumes,
As different fweets are yet perfumes.
Like Proteus, various fhapes it bears,
Graceful in various robes appears;
One while in fimple garb its feen,
Another,—tricked out like a queen.
In LONDON much falfe WIT is fold,
As Sheffield coin is pafs'd for gold!
And oft in WIT you're cheated there,
As you're deceiv'd in Wedgewood ware.
Thus priefts preach up their creeds for reafon,
And Liberty denounce as treafon.
So fpurious WITS for true ones fhine,
As Tories think a King divine.

* Received from Portfmouth, May 1, 1794.

'Tis not a tale which coxcombs tell,
Scarce underſtood beyond Pall-mall ;
Nor is it modiſh converſation,
Which deſerves that appellation ;
St. George's ſtar may deck the knight,
But ne'er can make a R*CH**ND fight.
—WIT lies not in a Frenchman's vapour,
Who helps his nonſenſe by a caper ;
In life by ſocial evils curſt,
A lively fool is ſure the worſt,
Vivacity lends dullneſs aid,
As lead by quickſilver's outweigh'd.—

Much leſs has that to WIT a claim,
Which makes a Virgin bluſh thro' ſhame ;
A bluſh ſweet apprehenſion ſhews,
The cheek then emulates the roſe.
If frigid Swift had lov'd the fair,
Their nice ſenſations he would ſpare.
The modeſt glow can they command ?
" They bluſh, becauſe they underſtand."
True ;—ſentiment their blood will rule,
The maid muſt bluſh, who's not a fool.—

Still may the dear fuffufion fhoot,
To tell the coxcomb, he's a brute.—

   No WIT is he, who oft rehearfes,
A few poor flimfy limping verfes;
Your ftanzas muft not only chime,
But fenfe refin'd keep pace with rhime,
As with their pafte, Cooks raifins mingle,
Rich thoughts muft knead with fterile jingle.
The proofs of WIT long while remain,
As ink will leave a lafting ftain.

   With WIT, your fpeech you fhould not load,
The Britons who made ufe of Woad,
Painted their bodies here and there,
But did not daub them every where.—
WIT on all points is out of feafon,
It's ufe is to embroider reafon.—
Good fenfe like cloth, the ground-work place,
And then fow on your WIT and lace.
The dome let Doric pillars prop,
Corinthian wreaths may grace the top.
The fabre's hilt with gems inlaid,
Give's luftre to the ufeful blade.

To guard the head the helmet wear,
The plume but adds a grace and air;
Kian, and Soy are good ingredients,
But for the turbot, poor expedients.
—Some hurt themfelves by flippant WIT,
As too much GAS, balloons will fplit;—
With buoyant fplendour, up they rife,
The fpirit burfts, the bubble dies.——

WIT lies not in Charards or pun,
Or what the grinning wag calls fun;
Nor can we find it on the ftage,
In C**BER**ND's, or C*WL*Y's page.
If SHERIDAN but fpeak or write,
WIT always beams a genuine light.—

By Locke, true WIT is beft defin'd,
Her pleafant pictures lure the mind;
Affociations fudden rife,
And feize the fancy by furprife;
The effect is ftrong,—becaufe it's odd,
Like fire electric from a clod;
Or when *fix'd* air puts out a light,
Tho' *vital* makes it blaze more bright.

Thus novelty a zeſt ſupplies,
And WIT ſtill pleaſes by ſurpriſe;
The brilliant thought that charm'd to day,
By repetition fades away;
A maid thus ſhines the joy of life;—
But what a different thing's a wife ?
WIT ſuits not the heroic line,
Her ſimiles are not divine;
The ludicrous they blithly ſeaſon,
And make us laugh in ſpite of reaſon:—
Diſcordant tho' the ideas be,
In Fancy's logic they agree;
As in the Ark by ſpecial grace,
Mice liv'd with Cats, yet throve apace.

TO EMMA,

ON HER BIRTH-DAY, MAY 5, 1792.

O F all the months that grace the varied year,
  What month so pleasant as the festive MAY!
When do the flowers so sweet and fresh appear,
  The fields so verdant, and the birds so gay.

Nature in concert seems at once to rise,
  From wintry darkness, and the gloom of night;
The Sun again illumes the purpled skies,
  And glads the world with his resplendent light.

Hail lovely MAY, beneath thy bounteous hand,
  Thy fost'ring vigilance, thy genial care;
The beauteous shrub and plant, their sweets expand,
  And with reviving fragrance scent the air.

Could I, like DRYDEN tune the vocal shell,
  Then would I sing the charms that MAY adorn;
Nor should the tender Muse forget to tell,
  That EMMA (fairest flower) in MAY was born.

VERSES ADDRESSED TO EMMA,

ON HER GOING TO WINDSOR.

———————

THE fplendid fcene that round you glows,
 Let EMMA's tafte difplay :
Where Thames the Prince of Rivers flows,
 Winding his filver way.

Beneath afpiring Windfor's height,
 The beauteous profpect lies ;
Here, verdant meadows charm the fight,
 There, tow'ring forefts rife.—

Hark ! Cowley fill'd with rapturous fire,
 Pours forth his lively fong ;
While Denham wakes his vocal lyre,
 To numbers fmooth and ftrong.

What ſtrains ſo ſoft, ſo ſweet and clear,
 On tuneful Zephyrs float?
The ſounds ſymphonious charm the ear,—
 'Tis Pope's enchanting note.

But in St. George's ſacred dome,
 What brilliant pageants ſhine!
There, *ribban'd* fools delighted roam,
 Bedeck'd by Kings divine.

Gay Charles's Fair adorn yon pile,
 With Zeuxis' Helen vie;
Like her diſplay the 'witching ſmile,
 And roll the ſleepy eye.

Let others prize your green retreats,
 Your vallies, meads, and hills;
Your terrace walk;—your tow'ring ſeats,
 Your ſtreams and purling rills.

Windſor, with theſe bright ſcenes you're bleſt;
 In Beauties you abound;
But ONE ſuperior to the reſt,
 Now treads your claſſic ground—

F

There EMMA fhines, with every grace,
  Good humour'd, blithe and gay;
And throws a luftre o'er each place,
  By wit's enchanting play.

VERSES ON AMBITION,

SUGGESTED BY AN ANECDOTE OF CÆSAR,

RELATED BY PLUTARCH.

⸻

As Cæsar once perus'd the warlike page,
    Big with the acts of Macedonia's chief;
Difcordant paffions in his bofom rage
    And fudden tears declare his inward grief.

His ardent friends around their leader preft,
    Whofe fervid looks indignant fiercenefs dart,—
The future tyrant then his foul exprefs'd,
    For luft of praife inflamed his daring heart.

" Ere PHILIP's godlike fon my years attain'd,
    " His triumphs o'er the earth's wide orb were fpread;
" Ambition's lofty feat the hero gain'd,
    " And conqueft twin'd her laurels round his head.

" While I remain unnotic'd and unknown,

    " A novice yet among the fons of fame;

" Where are the trophies I can call my own?

    " * What fpoils of victory can Cæfar claim?"

Thus Julius burning with ambition's fire,

    At length thro' Roman blood to empire rofe;

O ftill like Cæfar, may the wretch expire,

    Whofe fame upon his country's ruin grows.

May vengeful Heav'n the patriot † Chieftain blefs,

    Who nobly ftruggles in his country's caufe;

And crown his glorious labours with fuccefs,

    Who fights for freedom, and for equal laws.‡

---

* " Obferve with how much indifference Cæfar relates, in the Commentaries of the Gallic war; *that* he put to death the whole Senate of the Veneti, who had yielded to his mercy (iii. 16.) *that* he laboured to extirpate the whole nation of Eburenes, (vi. 31.) *that* forty thoufand perfons were maffacred at Bareges by the juft revenge of his foldiers, who fpared neither age nor fex. (vii. 27.)"——*Note, Gibbon's Hiftory, vol.* iv. *p.* 416. *Octavo Edition.*

† Ισονομ8ς τ' Αθηνας εποιησατον.
               Ode in Praife of Harmodius and Ariftogiton.

‡ The heroic Kosciousko.

But he who dares a people's rights invade,
    Who myriads for dominion would enslave;
May all his toils with infamy be paid;
    And *deep mouth'd* curses wait him to the grave.

In deep oblivion may his acts be hid,
    Nor let his victories be known to fame;
As Greece her sons to found his name forbid,
    Who fir'd a Temple to acquire a name.

Ask scepter'd Genius haft'ning to the tomb,
    If war's proud trophies, could such blifs impart,
As when he bid the village garden bloom,
    * And rais'd the COT to glad the peafant's heart?

As the fell lightning fires the lurid sky,
    So glares the VICTOR's momentary blaft;
While Virtue holds her glorious courfe on high,—
    Her mild effulgence will for ever laft.—

* " I never felt fo much pleafure, faid FREDERIC the Great, as in
" relieving the diftreffes of the peafants, and rebuilding their cottages."
Zimmerman's Converfations with the late King of Pruffia.

THE NUNS SONG.

―――――――――

No more we'll celebrate the mafs,
　　With Abbeffes and Friars;
But all our future moments pafs,
　　In foothing foft defires.

To nuptial blifs, we'll now afpire,
　　And beauty's triumph fhew;
While beam our eyes with youthful fire,
　　While yet our bofoms glow.——

To Venus, and the winged boy,
　　We'll dedicate our lives;
Chafte Nuns muft feel a double joy
　　As Mothers, and as Wives.

REPUBLICAN SONG.

IN triumph ſhall Liberty reign,
    And the Goddeſs expand all her charms,
If we hail her Republican ſtrain,
    That calls us to arms—and to arms !

Behold,—where the Auſtrians advance,
    Behold the tyrannical band;
How they ſwarm o'er the borders of France,
    And menace with ruin the land.

Then away,—to the frontiers away,
    And the legions of deſpots defy;
The voice of fair freedom obey,
    Determin'd to conquer, or die.

Crown'd with glory, victorious we'll reſt,
    And in triumph exultingly ſing ;—
That man, ſocial man may be bleſt,
    Without Nobles, or Biſhop, or King.—

THE PROPHET'S MISTAKE;

OR,

THE ILLUMINED TURNIP.

A COLLEGE EXERCISE.

CAMBRIDGE, FEBRUARY 10, 1793.

Credat Judæus Apella,
Non Ego

HOR.

Cætera mendacis deliramenta cataftæ,
Ne pueros ipfos credere poffe reor.

CLAUDII RUTILII ITER.

IT is I truft allow'd by all,
That great events proceed from fmall,
 From trifles oft arife;
As by experience 'tis found out,
That fnow-balls when they're roll'd about,
 Increafe in bulk and fize.

By fome I know 'tis deem'd a libel,
To doubt the ftories in the Bible,
  By prophet Mofes told;
Yet furely, many as related,
Are moft egregioufly miftated,
  Why not the truth unfold?

In Exodus 'tis fomewhere faid,
That Mofes as the flock he led,
  To Horeb's mountain came,
And while to reach its height he fteer'd,
An Angel wond'roufly appear'd
  Clad in a fiery flame.——

His eyes then upward Mofes turn'd,
A bufh with fire celeftial burn'd,
  And yet the bufh was whole;
The Jew was fill'd with vaft delight,
And cried, " I ne'er faw fuch a fight,
  " Upon my word 'tis droll."——

The bufh unfing'd continu'd flaming,
And while the Seer was thus exclaiming,

He heard a voice,—how odd!
Say, " Mofes, mark what I command,
" 'Tis holy ground on which you ftand,
    " Approach not while you're fhod!"

But when the voice moreover faid,
" I am the SIRE of Abraham dead,
    " And SIRE of Jacob too;"
Mofes began to quake apace,
And panic ftruck conceal'd his face,
    What elfe could Mofes do?

Ye fons of Ifrael mark the end,
Your ears I wifh not to offend,
    Nor heathenifh thoughts awake;
Altho' my bofom burns to tell,
How laughably your prophet fell,
    Into this droll miftake.—

Two boys to mifchief always quick,
Archly refolv'd to play a trick,
    On fome poor helplefs wight;
Tore from a neighbouring peafants' land,
A Turnip with flagitious hand,
    And hung there-on a light.

Then on a branch the Turnip hung,
Which as from fide to fide it fwung,

 The Legiflator ey'd;
Then turn'd, and looking with delight,
Confider'd it as grand a fight

 As ever man efpy'd.—

But when the boys began to fpeak,
Palenefs at once feiz'd Mofes' cheek,

 His blood with terror froze ;
But who can tell the Prophet's fear,
When they cry'd, " Mofes come not near,

 " Pull off your fhoes and hofe."

For fince he had no faith in ghofts,＊
He thought it thund'ring Jove—of Hofts,

 Who watch'd o'er Is-ra-el,
So ftrait he pen and paper took,
And in his memorandum book,

 Wrote down—a Mi-ra-cle !

Now, as the fecret I've difclos'd,
On Mofes, how two boys impos'd;

* See *Warburton's Divine Legation.*

By a device fo ftale;
Let's fagely on his annals pore,
We'll find by prying o'er and o'er,
   Full many a pleafant tale.

For inftance, left poor JONAS drown,
A Whale commiffion'd gulp'd him down,
   And lodg'd him to his wifh;
Where three whole days he fnugly ftaid,
Nor fix-pence for his chamber paid,
   To the good natur'd fifh.

Hail Bible, learned code of truth!
Thy tales fo fit for age or youth,
   In fimple guife are told;
As one drug giv'n in ten difeafes,
So this book every mortal pleafes,
   Young, middle aged, or old.—

EPIGRAM,

ON SEEING A GREAT OFFICER,
(LATELY RETURNED FROM FLANDERS)
DRIVING HIS PHAETON.

As from the hands of some infantine boy,

We snatch the scissars, and present a toy;

Thus Cæsar hails his Hero from the field,

And gives him Whips instead of swords to wield.

TO MRS. BLAIR,

ON HER COPYING SACHARISSA'S PICTURE.

———————

WHEN you, fam'd Sachariſſa's form diſplay,
Her glowing features with ſuch taſte pourtray,
Waller's bright love reſumes an air divine,
Her ſparkling eyes again with luſtre ſhine;
While o'er her neck the auburn ringlets flow,
And ſweetly wanton o'er a neck of ſnow.
Her blooming cheeks, and roſeate lips unite,
To fire the heart, entrance the raviſh'd ſight;
Such brilliant *traits* the beauteous tyrant grace,
And ſhed a radiance o'er her heav'nly face.

But in what brilliant circle ſhall we find,
Manners ſo poliſh'd, fancy ſo refin'd,

Such foft attractions, elegance and eafe,
A voice harmonious, ever tun'd to pleafe,
As in the Painter, whofe bewitching art
Revives the charms that won the Poet's heart.

THE END.